The Bear
Who Was Left
Behind

PAM AYRES

Illustrated by Nigel McMullen

BBC BOOKS

Mummy, Claire and James McPhee,
Went to a Teddy Bears' Picnic Tea.
There were lots of people there,
And children had to bring a bear.

There were bears of every size –
Different bodies, different eyes.
Some dressed up as him or her,
While some bears only wore their fur.

Claire had taken Snowy Bear,
Took her pram and wheeled him there.
James had brought his best bear, Fred,
The one he always took to bed.

At the Teddy Bears' Picnic Tea,
There were lots of things to see.
A man on stilts went wobbling by,
His head was right up in the sky!

A band was busy playing tunes,
There were ice-creams and balloons,
Sandwiches and rolls and cake,
And no-one had a tummyache!

A funny clown asked James and Claire,
If they had a cake to spare.
He waved it all around his ear,
And then he made it disappear!

But Mum kept glancing overhead,
"I think it's going to rain," she said.
And suddenly a heavy drop,
Splashed in Snowy's teacup – plop!

Then teeming rain fell on the place,
And stinging everybody's face,
People panicked everywhere,
And so did Mummy, James and Claire.

To the car they ran, all three,
With what was left of the picnic tea.
Coats and cups, the plate of ham,
Tomatoes, forks and Snowy's pram.

All the people drove away,
Rain had come and spoiled their day.
But out among the bits of bread,
Burst balloons and mud . . . lay Fred.

They'd forgotten Fred the Bear!
Driven off and left him there!
Staring upwards at the rain,
Listening for a car, in vain.

Back at home the truth was plain,
They searched for Fred and searched again.
They hunted low, they hunted high,
And James McPhee began to cry.

He cried to think of faithful Fred,
The bear he always took to bed,
Friendly Fred so warm and kind,
The Bear who had been left behind.

Dad came home and shook his head,
Nothing could be done, he said.
For it was now too wet and dark,
And much too late to search the Park.

So James McPhee got into bed,
James' heart was made of lead.
Beside him was an empty space,
And quiet tears ran down his face.

Through the window, right up high,
A friendly moon climbed in the sky.
Shining through the gloomy dark,
On the town, and on the Park.

The very Park where James McPhee,
Went for the Teddy Bears' Picnic Tea.
Moonlight shone on the locked-up gate,
It was lonely. It was late.

The saddest bear in all the land,
Fred, who'd slipped from James' hand,
Wide awake and stiff with fright,
Heard the noises of the night.

Massive cows came squelching through,
Nosed at Fred and sniffed and blew.
And something with a stripy face,
Softly padded past the place.

There were rabbits, there were deer,
A fox's eyes, alert and clear.
A bat swooped down and a weasel whined:
"Some old bear's been left behind."

The sound of someone breathing fast!
A man in shadow running past!
Fred could see the heavy sack
He carried, bouncing, on his back.

Hidden in the trees so tall,
An owl peered down upon them all.
Saw the black sky turn to grey,
As night began to ebb away.

Morning came so cold and clear,
Then slowly, surely, drawing near,
The nicest sound he'd heard so far,
Fred the Bear could hear . . . A CAR!

Slowly, slowly, down the track,
Faces peered from front and back.
Oh *was* it James? Was this car his?
Then voices shouted, "There he is!"

Voices Fred had longed to hear,
Racing feet were coming near,
And Fred the Bear looked up to see,
Mummy, Claire and James McPhee!

James, who had been so upset,
Picked up Fred all soaking wet,
Gently wrapped him in a towel,
Hugged him tight and made him growl.

Washed and dried and brushed went Fred,
Deep in James' cosy bed,
And thought "For next year's Picnic Tea,
I hope James will not choose ME!"

Published by BBC Books,
a division of BBC Enterprises Limited,
Woodlands, 80 Wood Lane, London W12 0TT
First published 1991
© Pam Ayres 1991
ISBN 0 563 36209 X
Illustrations © Nigel McMullen
Set in Plantin Roman by Goodfellow and Egan Ltd, Cambridge
Printed and bound in Belgium by Proost NV
Colour separations by DOT Gradations Ltd, Chelmsford
Paper case printed by Proost NV